HECTOR
HELICOPTER

Written and illustrated
by
ARTHUR W. BALDWIN

DEAN

First published by Dean & Son Ltd 1964
Copyright © 1964 Reed International Books Ltd
First published in the UK in this edition 1994 by Dean,
an imprint of Reed Children's Books,
Michelin House, 81 Fulham Road, London SW3 6RB
and Auckland, Melbourne, Singapore and Toronto

ISBN 0603 556 027
Printed and Bound in the UK

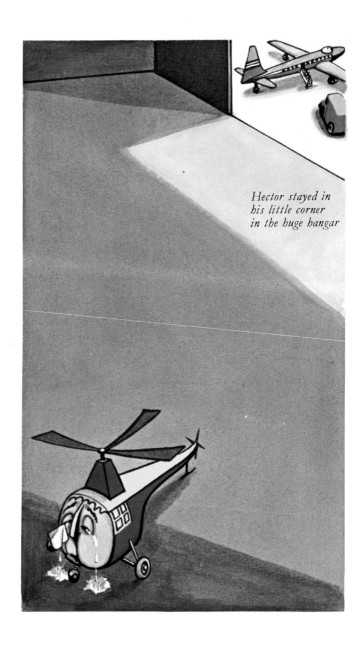

Hector stayed in his little corner in the huge hangar

HECTOR THE HELICOPTER

Hector the Helicopter lived in a hangar with lots of other aeroplanes. Big aeroplanes they were, too, that travelled to all the exciting places in the world.

Sometimes they were away for days and days, while Hector stayed in his little corner in the huge hangar, unwanted and forgotten.

This made him very unhappy.

When the big planes came back, they would talk together and tell one another of their journeys—the great cities they had visited, the wide seas they had flown over, and the aerodromes they had stopped at in the far-off lands where the sun was hot and the skies were very blue. The big aeroplanes took no notice of Hector at all.

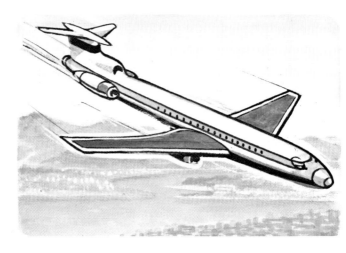

They were much too important to talk to a very small helicopter.

"Really," sneered a huge jet airliner, when he happened to notice Hector one day. "I can't think what use these little things are. They go straight up into the air and travel about as fast as a horse and cart." The jet plane laughed unpleasantly, while the others looked down their long noses with disdain at poor Hector.

He shrank back farther into his corner while the tears rolled down his cheeks.

"One day," he sobbed quietly to himself, "I'll show them I *am* useful. I will do something they can't do." But he had no idea what he was going to do, or when he would do it.

*The jet plane
laughed unpleasantly*

Hector went to sleep that night and dreamed he was flying fast and high over mountains that were made of sugar plum pudding, circled by wide rivers of clear sparkling lemonade.

Hector woke from his wonderful dream to hear the roar of engines just outside the hangar. He looked around him, only half awake.

The hangar was quite empty. Hector knew then that the roaring engines he could hear was the last of the big planes about to start on one of its long and exciting journeys.

How he wished he was an airliner instead of a very small helicopter. How he would like to visit Paris, Rome, Baghdad, Australia, or Hong-Kong. Nothing exciting like that ever happened to him.

"I am not going to stay in this dark old

He dreamed he was flying over mountains made of sugar plum pudding

corner any longer," said Hector to himself. "I am going out, too."

Hector rolled himself to the door of the hangar and peeped out. It was just beginning to get light. Standing on the runway was one of the big airliners, its engines roaring. It was almost ready to take off. This was his chance!

Before Hector quite knew what he was doing, he was out of the hangar. Quietly he rolled himself to the small field at the back of the airfield.

Everyone was too busy with the airliner to notice a small helicopter rise into the air and make off towards the rising sun.

Everyone was too busy to notice a small helicopter rise into the air

"Oh dear!" thought Hector. "I will get into awful trouble when I get back." But as he went up and up and on and on, the naughty little helicopter forgot all about the aerodrome and the dark corner in the hangar.

He was just beginning to enjoy himself in the lovely morning air when a great roaring, hissing sound came from behind him. It got closer and closer. Then WH-E-E-E-E-E—Z-Z-Z-Z-Z—H-I-S-S-S!

Poor Hector was almost deafened as a wicked-looking fighter-jet shot past, and quite close to him, at a terrific speed.

Hector spluttered and coughed as the smoke and vapour from the fighter covered him.

He was very frightened too.

"I—I do h-hope h-he doesn't come back," quavered Hector as he turned as quickly as

Hector spluttered and coughed

his propeller would twist him and headed off in the other direction.

As he buzzed along in the clear morning sky, Hector soon got over his fright.

"This is better than being shut up in that old hangar," he laughed.

Below him the fields and hedges looked beautiful and green. In the distance he could see the sea shining and sparkling in the morning sunlight.

"I have not been to the seaside for a long time," he told himself. "Perhaps I will be able to sit on the sands and paddle my wheels in the water. That will be fun."

Squawk! Squawk! Whatever is that noise?

"It's only me," squawked
a seagull

It came again, louder this time. SQUAWK!
S-Q-U-A-W-K! Hector's engine missed a
beat. "It is that horrible fighter-jet coming
back," he thought.

"It's only me," squawked a seagull. "Don't
be frightened, I will not hurt you."

"I am not afraid," said Hector, "but your
claws are tickling my nose. Please come farther
down my back, then I can hear you better."

The seagull edged himself closer to Hector's
ear. "I want your help," rasped out the seagull.
"There are two sailors shipwrecked on the
rocks off the point. Do you think you can
rescue them?"

Hector was all action now. He was glad that
he had not taken off his lifting ropes when he

Two men were waving a piece of white cloth

ran away from the aerodrome. They were still fastened to his under-wheel.

"Show me the way," he called to the seagull, as they both headed seawards.

As they crossed the point, Hector could see two men waving a piece of white cloth on the top of the rocks about a mile out to sea.

"We will have to hurry," shouted the seagull. "The tide's coming in fast and the sea will cover the rocks." Then he left Hector and flew to the rocks.

Hector's engine roared to full speed and very soon he was circling round the two ship-wrecked sailors. At the same time he lowered his lifting ropes so that they dangled just above the rocks. As the ropes touched the place where the sailors were clinging, Hector slowed down his engine and hovered over them.

The first man grabbed the rope

There was quite a com-
motion when Hector got
back to the aerodrome

He felt a sharp tug as the first sailor grabbed
e rope and climbed. He quickly scrambled
to Hector's cabin. Then the second sailor
d the same. They were rescued from the sea.
s Hector turned to fly back to land, his
iend, the seagull, sailed alongside and
uawked in his ear. "Hector, you are a hero!"
There was quite a commotion when Hector
ot back to the aerodrome. Everyone said
hat a good job he had done and what a fine
llow he was.
No one said anything about being away
hen he should have been in his hangar.
Hector thought it would be a good thing
he went back to his little corner before
meone remembered he had played truant.
But no one did! He was the hero of the

aerodrome. When the long-distance airliner came back and heard about Hector's adventure and rescue, they, too, said what a fine fellow he was. They no longer looked down their noses at him, but told him stories of their adventures and travels.

This made Hector very happy. Even the huge Boeing jet-liner joined in praise of him.

"We may be able to fly at hundreds of miles an hour," he said one morning, "but we can't fly straight up and down like Hector can."

"Nor can we keep still in the air and rescue people from rocks," joined in another.

All the other planes agreed and sang "For he's a jolly good fellow".

That is how Hector the Helicopter became Hector the Hero.